www.carameltree.com

Same Day Sunday

Chapter 1
The First Sunday

It was Sunday morning. Jon sat at his desk. The window was open. He felt the wind on his face and smelled the sea air.

Jon had to write about turtles for homework, but he could not think of anything to write. He chewed the top of his pencil and stared at the blank page.

The sound of the waves on the beach was too much. He dropped his pencil and looked up. *'I'll go to the beach for an hour,'* he thought, *'my homework can wait.'*

Jon saw Ben and Ella on their surfboards.

"Where have you been?" asked Ben.

"I was doing my homework," said Jon, "I'll finish it later."

Jon played in the waves and then he lay on his towel.

"What shall we do now?" Ben asked.

"Let's get ice-cream," Ella said. "Then we can go fishing. Dad's on the dock."

The afternoon went quickly. The kids caught many fish.

"Look kids!" shouted Ella's dad. "There's a turtle."

"I don't like turtles," said Jon.

"Why?" asked Ben.

"I have to write about turtles for my homework," said Jon.

Ella's dad laughed. "I'm sure you would like turtles if you knew more about them," he said. "Why don't you all come back to our house? I'll cook your fish on the barbecue."

'I don't like fish,' thought Jon, *'but anything is better than doing homework.'*

Chapter 2
Mixed-up?

The next morning, Jon woke up and stretched. He took a shower, got dressed, and went into the kitchen.

Jon ate a bowl of cereal and wondered why the house was quiet. Where was everybody? Why wasn't Lucy screaming in her highchair?

After breakfast, Jon went to his parents' bedroom. He knocked quietly on the door.

"Yes, who's there?" said Mom in a sleepy voice.

"It's 7 o'clock! Time to get up!" Jon shouted.

"It's Sunday," said Dad, "go back to bed, Jon."

'They're mixed-up,' thought Jon.

Jon picked up his school bag and left the house.

On the way to school, he met Ella and Ben. They were carrying their surfboards.

"Where are you going?" asked Ella.

"To school," Jon answered.

Ella and Ben looked at each other and laughed.

"Are you crazy?" said Ben. "It's Sunday!"

Jon didn't believe his friends. He left them and walked to school.

When Jon arrived at school, he found the gates locked. There was no one at school.

Somewhere nearby, a church bell rang.

'Okay, it must be Sunday,' Jon decided. 'Yesterday must have been Saturday.' He turned around and walked back home.

At home, Jon sat at his desk. He searched on the Internet to find a picture of a sea turtle. He copied the picture.

The window was open. The sound of the waves on the beach was too much. *'I'll go to the beach for an hour,'* thought Jon. *'I can finish my homework later.'*

At the beach, Ella and Ben were playing in the waves. Jon joined them. Afterwards, they bought ice-cream. Then they fished off the dock. Ella's dad pointed at a turtle under the dock. Jon ignored the turtle.

'Strange,' thought Jon. *'Today feels just the same as yesterday.'*

At the end of the day, Ella's dad cooked their fish on the barbecue.

'Not fish again,' thought Jon. 'Why can't we have burgers?'

Later at home, Jon sat at his desk. 'I don't know anything about turtles,' he thought to himself. He put his head on his desk. He was tired from playing at the beach so he went to sleep.

The next morning, Jon woke up. He packed his school bag, took a shower, and got dressed. He went into the kitchen, but no one was there.

Jon knocked on his parents' door.

"Yes," Mom called, "who's there?"

"It's 7 o'clock! Time to get up!" Jon shouted.

"It's Sunday," said Dad, in a sleepy voice, "go back to bed, Jon."

Jon felt sick. Not *another* Sunday. It *couldn't* be Sunday. He had already had two Sundays in a row.

'This is getting boring,' thought Jon. 'Where did Monday and Tuesday go?'

Jon had a fourth Sunday, a fifth Sunday, and then a sixth. He was sick of Sundays. He was sick of not getting his homework done.

Chapter 4
Sick of Sundays

On the seventh Sunday, Jon sat at his desk, stared at the turtle drawing, and thought. *'Nothing changes. Every day is the same. Every day is Sunday.'*

Jon talked to Mom. "I'm sick of Sundays," he said. "We've had seven Sundays in a row!"

"That imagination of yours," laughed Mom. "What will you think of next?"

Jon talked to Ella and Ben. "Aren't you sick of Sundays?" he asked. "We've had seven Sundays in a row!"

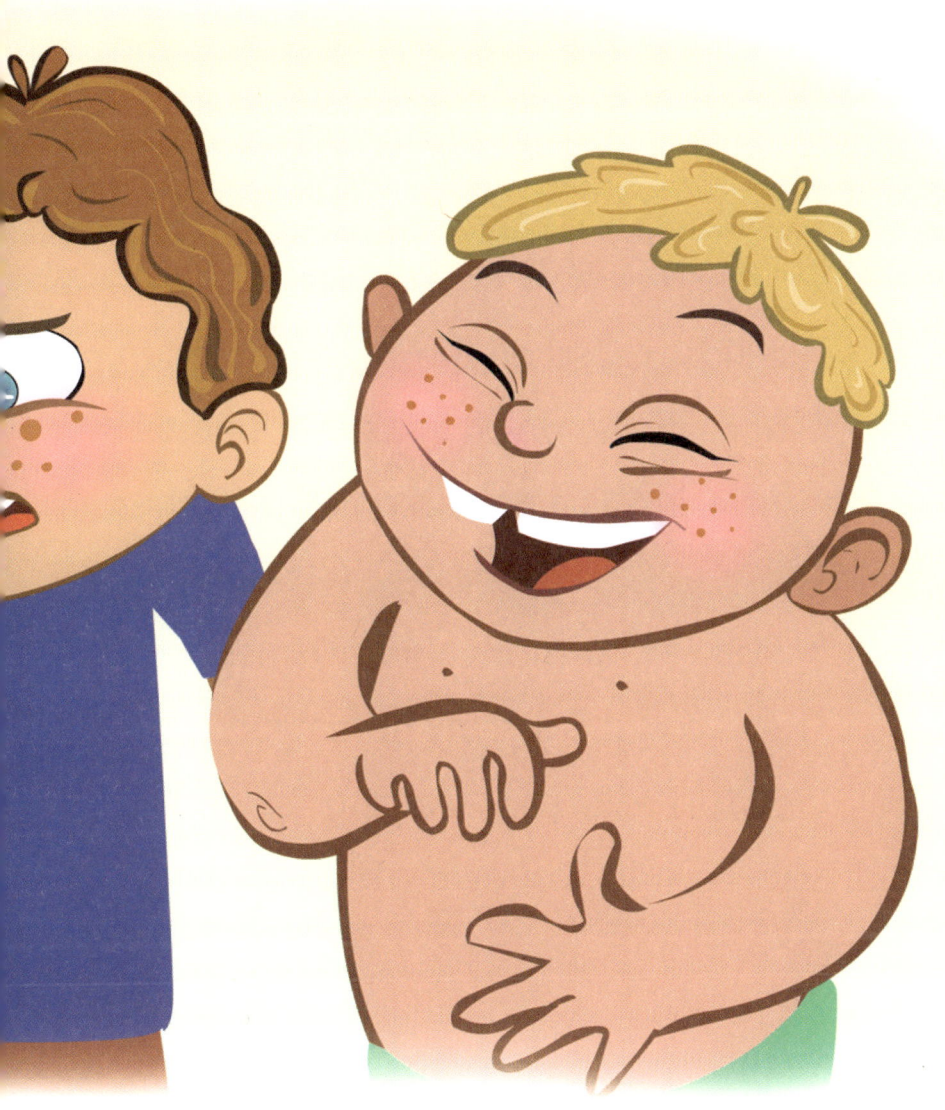

"I wish it was true," Ben laughed.

"I'd love every day to be a Sunday," said Ella. "Then there would be no more school."

The kids played on the beach and then they fished off the dock. Ella's dad pointed at the turtle, just like he had on all the other Sundays.

"I wish I knew more about turtles," said Jon. "Then I could finish my homework."

"Sea turtles are interesting," said Ella's dad, and he told Jon everything he knew about them.

Jon listened carefully. There was so much to know about turtles.

Later at home, Jon sat at his desk. This is what he wrote:

The sea turtle is the same size as me. It is about 1 meter long, but it weighs much more than I do. The sea turtle can swim faster than I can. It can swim up to 30 kilometers an hour.

A sea turtle can get very old. It can live up to 50 years old. It can sleep underwater…

Jon yawned.

…and stayed there for a few hours.

Chapter 5
Monday, Finally

The next morning, Jon woke up and stretched. He stopped for a moment and wondered if it was Sunday again.

"Hurry up, Jon," Mom called. "You'll be late for school."

"What?" said Jon. He jumped out of bed and ran downstairs in his pajamas. "What day is it?"

"It's Monday, of course," said Dad. "What day did you think it was?" he asked.

"It doesn't matter," said Jon, "as long as it isn't Sunday!"

Jon ran back upstairs to get ready for school. He was happy he had finished his homework. Most of all, he was happy he could finally go to school again.